Lani: The Nomad Coqui and the Sea of Stars

Sara Gavrell Ortiz

Illustrator: Christie López

2024

© Sara Gavrell Ortiz
© Editora Educación Emergente, 2024-2029

Translation: Sara Gavrell Ortiz
Copy Editing: Beatriz Llenín Figueroa
Illustrations: Christíbiri López
Cover Design: Nelson Vargas Vega
Book Design: Lissette Rolón Collazo

ISBN-13: 979-8-3507-2831-6

Series: *Otra escuela*

Editora Educación Emergente, Inc.
Alturas de Joyuda #6020
C/Stephanie
Cabo Rojo, PR 00623-8907
editora@editoraemergente.com
www.editoraemergente.com

Printed at Extreme Graphics
Naguabo, Puerto Rico

HUMANIDADES
PUERTO RICO
CENTRO PARA EL LIBRO

NATIONAL
ENDOWMENT
FOR THE
HUMANITIES

15
ANIVERSARIO
2009-2024

#LiberaTuLectura

To the coquís of La Finca, to my adored mother,
Naida Ortiz Santiago, who raised me there, and to my daughter,
my delicious Artemisa, for whom I wrote this story:
The world is for playing.

Lani, the coquí, wanted to travel and have adventures. More than anything, Lani wanted to see the sea. Her grandmother, who had been a professor and spoke of strange things, said the sea was an infinite puddle. Lani, who loved water, could not believe it. "An infinite puddle of water that you cannot jump?" She thought.

Lani loved to play pirates with her best friend Nicolás.

"The wind is picking up. Raise the sail. Let's go have adventures!" — Lani would say.

"Yes, my captainess! Churí churí qui qui qui!" —Nicolás would answer. Traversing the infinite puddle seemed like the most exciting thing in the world.

One day, Lani was woken up by an uproar. The humans were unearthing all the green bromeliads that formed her community! While the coquís were getting ready to move to the red bromeliads, Lani snuck out and climbed into the human's truck.

Lani's heart was racing. "I am going to have adventures! Then I'll come back and tell Nicolás everything," she thought.

When the truck stopped, Lani thought she was on top of the world. She could feel a light rain and smell the humidity. Her eyes traced the immensity of the mountains and the sky. Though it wasn't dark yet, she could see the moon. Lani could hear a multitude of insects, birds, and coquís. And in the middle of everything, there was a huge white plate.

Lani climbed onto the white plate where a coquí was singing.
"Hi. My name is Felipe. What's yours? I've never seen you around here.
And I know eeeeeveryone." —Said the coquí.

"My name is Lani. And I am looking for the sea." —Lani answered.
"The sea? I've never seen it. I think it's far." —Felipe said.
Felipe told her the white plate was the biggest telescope in the world.
"The humans use it to talk to the people in space." —Felipe said.

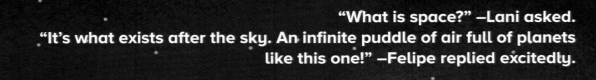

"What is space?" —Lani asked.
"It's what exists after the sky. An infinite puddle of air full of planets like this one!" —Felipe replied excitedly.

Lani was fascinated.
"Can you be a space pirate?" —Lani asked.
"I imagine so. Come on, let's skate!" —Exclaimed Felipe.
"So cool! I've never skated before!" —Replied Lani with a big smile.

There was a big party that night. Felipe introduced her to eeeeeveryone and played his guitar, while they skated, danced, and sang coquí coquí co qui qui ri qui! churí churí qui qui qui!
At dawn, Lani went to say goodbye to Felipe.

"Why don't you stay here to live with us? It's always fun and you will always have bromeliads." —Felipe said.
Lani was tempted to stay in that amazing mountain. But adventure was calling her, and she decided to leave.

Lani was able to jump on a motorcycle (which was super-fast!) that stopped in front of a vast cave with a river. Lani, who loved water, went to the riverbank and started singing "churí churí qui qui qui!" Then, she noticed a lizard was watching her.

"Hi. Do you want me to take you for a ride on the river? We can build a canoe."
—Said Juanita, the lizard.

Lani said yes immediately. Juanita collected a bunch of twigs and together they built a canoe.

Hold on! Though if you fall, it's really cool." —Said Juanita.
"The wind is picking up. Raise the sail. Let's go have adventures!" —Shouted Lani.
"Yes, my captainess!" —Juanita replied. Lani missed Nicolás a little.
Lani fell down the waterfalls "woo-hoo!" and she had a blast.

Before going to bed, Juanita asked: "Why don't you stay here to live with us? It's always fun and you can always play pirate in the caves."
Lani was tempted to stay in that fantastic forest. But adventure was calling her, and she decided to leave.

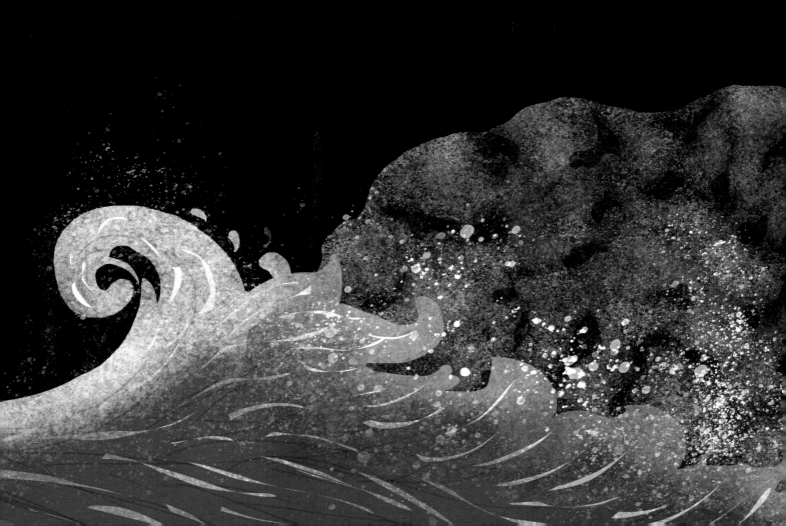

Lani hitched a car ride and arrived at a beach. She jumped on the warm sand and saw the sea. It was exactly as her grandmother had described it, an infinite puddle of water!

She went to the rocks by the shore.
"Hi, little one." —Said an enormous hawksbill turtle called Gurutze.

"Hello." —Said Lani. "I've always wanted to see the sea. It's full of blue sun. It's incredible."
"It's even more incredible underwater. Come with me." —Said Gurutze.
"But I can't breathe underwater." —Lani said.
"Don't worry. You can see everything from my shell." —Replied Gurutze.

Lani climbed onto Gurutze's shell and saw a marvelous world. A highway of colorful corals full of hawksbill turtles, fish, and octopuses.

"This is the most beautiful place I've ever seen!" —Exclaimed Lani.

"I am always travelling, and the most beautiful place I've ever seen is the sea of stars." —Said Gurutze.

"A sea of stars? I could be a space pirate! Will you take me there?" —Asked Lani excitedly.

They set sail at dawn.

"The wind is picking up. Raise the sail. Let's go have adventures!" —Said Lani.
"Yes, my captainess!" —Answered Gurutze.

Lani traversed the infinite puddle of water in her shell ship.

When they got to the bay, Gurutze bid farewell saying, "You are lucky.
Today is a new moon."

Soon it was dark. Lani questioned her decision. She had travelled far, she missed
Nicolás, and the black water did not look friendly.

Suddenly, a coquí jumped into the water with an explosion of light. Lani also
jumped. She was enveloped in shiny green light. She was swimming in the stars.

Lani and her new coquí friend, Leire, played pirates in space, going from
planet to planet, looking for adventures.

After their swim, the coquís of the bay made a fire, told stories about the wonders of the world, and sang "coquí coquí!" "churí churí!"

"Why don't you stay here to live with us? It's always fun and you can always be a space pirate." —Leire said.

"Well, I'll stay until tomorrow." —Lani replied.

Super!" —Leire answered. "I'll ask you the same thing tomorrow so that you answer the same thing!"

They started laughing.

Lani knew that adventure would soon call her.

She also had to go back to tell Nicolás.

Places in the Story

The University of Puerto Rico's Faculty Residences ("La Resi" o "La Finca") was for many years a housing community for national and international professors.

The Arecibo Observatory was built in 1960, and was the largest radio telescope in the world until 2016, when China finished its Five-hundred-meter Aperture Spherical Radio Telescope. The Arecibo Observatory collapsed on December 1st of 2020.

The Camuy River Cave National Park is the third largest cave network on the planet and the largest in the Western Hemisphere.

Tres Palmas Marine Reserve in Rincón was established in 2004 through a community-driven effort to protect marine biodiversity. It contains some of the healthiest Elkhorn Corals (classified as a "critically endangered" species) in the Caribbean.

The Bioluminescent Bay in Vieques, or Mosquito Bay, is the brightest in the planet, and was suggested as one of the Seven Wonders of the World by Condé Nast Traveler in 2020.

Christíbiri López is a graphic artist and illustrator from Puerto Rico, and just like Lani, she loves going on adventures with her dog, seeking inspiration in nature. She currently works for Ediciones SM, creating books for young people in her country. You can find her on Instagram at @christibiri_ilustra and reach her via email at cclopezsoy@gmail.com.

Recent Titles
Editora Educación Emergente

Ruinas, basura y menudo
René Duchesne Sotomayor
ISBN: 979-8-3507-2837-8

Todo pasa
Sofía Irene Cardona
ISBN: 979-8-3507-1826-3

Blanco Temblor
Carola García López
ISBN: 979-8-3507-1830-0

La niña y la mosca
Ileana Contreras Castro y Vicky Ramos (ilustradora)
ISBN: 979-8-3507-1823-2

¿Ojos que no ven? Colonialidad y cimarronaje visual en la República Dominicana
Rosa Elena Carrasquillo
ISBN: 979-8-3507-1825-6

*En mi celda: escritos desde la cárcel*Martin Sostre
Selección, edición y estudio por Julio Ramos
Traducido por Juan Carlos Quiñones, Paula Contreras y Julio Ramos
ISBN: 979-8-3507-1824-9

Borinquen Field
Marta Aponte Alsina
ISBN: 979-8-3507-1821-8

¡Juntes por la justicia climática!/Together for Climate Justice!
VV.AA.
ISBN: 979-8-3507-1822-5

Huerto de papel: ABC para una educación agroecológica inclusiva
Paola A. González Santiago
ISBN: 979-8-3507-0915-5